What did you say?
What do you mean?

also by Jude Welton and illustrated by Jane Telford

Can I tell you about Asperger Syndrome?
A guide for friends and family
Jude Welton
Illustrated by Jane Telford
ISBN 1 84310 206 4

of related interest

An Asperger Dictionary of Everyday Expressions
Ian Stuart-Hamilton
ISBN 1 84310 152 1

Freaks, Geeks and Asperger Syndrome
A User Guide to Adolescence
Luke Jackson
ISBN 1 84310 098 3

Asperger's Syndrome
A Guide for Parents and Professionals
Tony Attwood
ISBN 1 85302 577 1

Asperger Syndrome – What Teachers need to Know
Matt Winter
ISBN 1 84310 143 2

What did you say?
What do you mean?

An illustrated guide
to understanding metaphors

Jude Welton

Illustrated by Jane Telford

Foreword by Elizabeth Newson

Jessica Kingsley Publishers
London and New York

The right of Jude Welton to be identified as author of this work has been asserted by her in accordance with the Copyright, Designs and Patents Act 1988.

First published in the United Kingdom in 2004
by Jessica Kingsley Publishers Ltd
116 Pentonville Road
London N1 9JB, England
and
29 West 35th Street, 10th fl.
New York, NY 10001-2299, USA

www.jkp.com

Library of Congress Cataloging in Publication Data
A CIP catalog record for this book is available from the Library of Congress

British Library Cataloguing in Publication Data
A CIP catalogue record for this book is available from the British Library

ISBN 1 84310 207 2

Printed and Bound in Great Britain by
Athenaeum Press, Gateshead, Tyne and Wear

To JJ, the apple of my eye. (JW)
Ditto. (JT)

Contents

Acknowledgements   xii

Foreword by Elizabeth Newson   xiii

Introduction for children   xv

The illustrated metaphors   1

The metaphors are arranged alphabetically, based on the first noun – if there is one. If there is no noun, then the order is taken from the main word that doesn't change, such as "backwards" in "bend over backwards" (people sometimes say "lean over backwards").

1   The apple of your eye

2   Bend over backwards

3   Have a ball

4   On the ball

5   The ball is in your court

6   Start the ball rolling

7   Scrape the bottom of the barrel

8   Full of beans

9   Spill the beans

10   Get out of the wrong side of the bed

11   Rings a bell

12   Drive someone round the bend

13   Miss the boat

14   Rock the boat

15   A bone to pick with you

16   Don't judge a book by its cover

17   Too big for your boots

18   Cross that bridge when you come to it

19   Take the bull by the horns

20   Butterflies in your tummy

21   Carry the can

22   Open a can of worms

23   Burn the candle at both ends

24   Lay your cards on the table

25   Let the cat out of the bag

26   Raining cats and dogs

27   A big cheese

28   Don't count your chickens

29   A chip on your shoulder

30   That's the way the cookie crumbles

31   Too many cooks spoil the broth

32   Send someone to Coventry

33   Not your cup of tea

34   Call it a day

35   Don't put all your eggs in one basket

36   Walk on eggshells

37   Thrown in at the deep end

38   Make ends meet

39   Find your feet

40   Land on your feet

41   Sit on the fence

42   Keep your fingers crossed

43 Put your finger on it

44 Wrap someone around your little finger

45 Play with fire

46 A big fish in a small pond

47 Plenty more fish in the sea

48 A frog in your throat

49 Move the goalposts

50 Teach your grandmother to suck eggs

51 Lend a hand

52 Fly off the handle

53 Keep it under your hat

54 Bury the hatchet

55 Head in the clouds

56 Do that standing on your head

57 Speak off the top of your head

58 Bite your head off

59 Bury your head in the sand

60 Straight from the horse's mouth

61 Break the ice

62 Take a leaf out of someone's book

63 Turn over a new leaf

64 Pull your leg

65 Draw a line under it

66 A square meal

67 Change your mind

68 Over the moon

69 Face the music

70 Hit the nail on the head

71 Pie in the sky

72 Eat humble pie

73 A lot on your plate

74 Get the sack

75 Come out of your shell

76 Get your skates on

77 A skeleton in your cupboard

78 Something up your sleeve

79 A snake in the grass

80 Pull your socks up

81 The last straw

82 Draw the short straw

83 The straw that broke the camel's back

84 Swings and roundabouts

85 Hold your tongue

86 On the tip of your tongue

87 Long in the tooth

88 Bark up the wrong tree

89 Change your tune

90 Drive someone up the wall

91 Water off a duck's back

92 Water under the bridge

93 Feel under the weather

94 Pull your weight

95 A wolf in sheep's clothing

96 Not out of the woods

97 Pull the wool over someone's eyes

98 Get a word in edgeways

99 Take the words right out of someone's mouth

100 On top of the world

Blank pages for you to add to your
   metaphor collection   101

For parents and teachers

Appendix 1: A guide to helping children with
   Asperger Syndrome to understand what we mean   107

Appendix 2: Ideas for using this book   111

Acknowledgements

I would like to thank Elizabeth Newson, who first introduced me to the world of autism many years ago. A student couldn't ask for a more inspiring, sympathetic teacher. And when autism touched my life more closely than I could have expected, Elizabeth remained an equally inspiring and sympathetic friend, mentor and advocate. Her encouragement and suggestions gave me the confidence to see this book to its completion.

Thanks too to Eileen Griffith, my son's educational psychologist, for her comments and suggestions, and for the unfailing support she gives children with autistic spectrum disorders in our area. I'd like to thank Carol Gray, whose Social Stories have taught me so much, and which continue to help my son.

Thanks to Sally Smith, Anne McLean and Joyce Mason for their input. Thanks to Charlotte Gilbert, who – along with my son – helped me decide how to present the metaphors. Thanks to Jessica for saying "yes", and for everyone at JKP for all their help. A huge thank you to Jane for her enthusiasm and her wonderful illustrations.

But most of all, my love and thanks go to my husband David for his help and support with this project and with so much else, and to JJ, our lovely son, who inspired this book.

Foreword

I suppose one of the most surprising and difficult things for parents to get used to in learning to live with a young child who has Asperger Syndrome is what it really means (to them and their child) to be "inflexible". Every family has its own funny but rueful stories to tell. The stories are funny because you'd be crying if you didn't laugh; but they're rueful because we all recognize how truly handicapping this degree of rigidity must be to our child's personality and growth, and that we ourselves can't just shrug it off as an inconvenience.

For instance, we're all used to the idea that most children will try to filch an extra 20 minutes of television time before bedtime, or see how long they can make "one more story" last; but what if your child has such unbreakable rules for himself that getting home one minute late is going to involve an hour's stamping and screaming? What if his sister also "has to" obey his rule that only perfect biscuits may be eaten, but not by her? Parents of an autistic child as young as two years old can find themselves on a rapid learning curve about recognizing the very real distress that their child experiences when they accidentally break his self-imposed rules of behaviour. Where there are siblings to be thought of as well, making space for what we used to think of as normal family life can seem impossible in the face of "insistence on sameness" exerted over everyone else by the child with autism.

Children who have Asperger Syndrome usually have the great advantage of verbal ability. This doesn't necessarily mean that they are good communicators, because their poor social empathy makes them fail to notice whether others are making sense of what they are trying to say or are even listening. But they do have the skills of vocabulary and grammar that enable them to put together good sentences which they expect others to understand.

The trouble is that verbal communication is usually more complicated than that. First, we tend to talk to each other in a great variety of ways, listening to each other as we go along and trying to make what we say more interesting. Second, and perhaps especially in English, the way we talk is full of vivid "figures of speech" and visual images, which makes what we say much more lively but also more ambiguous: we play guessing games with each other about what we mean, but we are able to do that easily because of our strong social empathy about what we might mean, which allows us to get it right most of the time. So it probably won't be much of a problem if someone says, "Come on, pull your socks up, get cracking!" or "Keep it under your hat," or even "She was over the moon."

But all of this is so much more difficult for a child with Asperger's, who desperately tries to interpret what he hears in a rigid and literal way, maybe protesting angrily, "Don't say it wrong!" when he can't make head or tail (WHAT did you say?) of what his parents and teachers mean. No wonder some parents do their best to avoid using metaphors in their child's hearing, when they clearly cause him so much confusion.

But trying to avoid the forms of speech that come naturally is not really a realistic option, especially in the long term. What Jude Welton has given us here is a truly helpful introduction into the world of metaphor, rich enough to make it clear to the child what metaphors are all about, and how he could join in. To be honest, when we first tried to give children their own metaphoric repertoires, we didn't really have much hope of success. But we soon found that metaphors could have their own fascination for a child with Asperger's, once he got used to the idea that grownups could "mean what they said" in this very strange – and laughable – way. Humour helps; and Jude and Jane have given us plenty of that. The children we worked with on metaphor had a lot of fun adding to their own repertories, and eventually even experimenting to make up their own as the occasion required.

If we had had a book like this to inspire us, it would have given us a kick-start (a WHAT?). Any parent or teacher working with Asperger's will find it beginning to open the doors of imagination for the child in ways that they might not have thought possible. A lovely and practical book, which children and grownups can enjoy – and giggle over – together.

– Elizabeth Newson
Early Years Diagnostic Centre, Nottingham

Introduction for children

Sometimes words mean exactly what they say. This is called the words' literal meaning.

Sometimes words or phrases have a different meaning from this literal meaning. That's OK, but it might make you feel muddled.

For example, if someone says, "He's let the cat out of the bag," they don't usually mean that someone has literally let a cat escape from a bag. They mean that he has let other people know something that was meant to be kept a secret.

If someone says, "She'll bite your head off," they don't mean that the person will literally bite anyone's head off. What the speaker means is that the person is likely to be so annoyed that she speaks in an angry, "snappy" way.

If someone says, "I've changed my mind," they don't mean that they have got a different brain from the one they had before! They mean that they thought one way about something at first, and then they thought differently about it. They might say, "I didn't feel like going to the park this morning, but I've changed my mind. I would really like to go now."

Expressions such as these that don't mean literally what they say are called metaphors. A metaphor is a saying or expression whose meaning comes from a suggested comparison with something else. Metaphors usually create a picture in your mind. People use them to make language and conversation more interesting.

Using words in this way can be fun, but it can be confusing. Sometimes, you might feel upset if you don't understand what someone means when they use a metaphor to tell you or ask you something. If you don't understand what they mean, it's OK to ask them to explain.

This book will teach you 100 sayings that don't mean literally what they say. If I know why a saying has a particular meaning, I will tell you. For example, on page 25 you'll find out where the meaning of "to let the cat out of the bag" comes from. Sometimes, no one knows why a saying means what it does, so I can't tell you.

I hope you have fun learning metaphors. I hope you enjoy using them sometimes, and collecting new ones. There are some empty pages at the back of the book, so that you can add new sayings to your collection when you hear or read them. As you will see, there is a frame on each of these pages. You can draw your own illustrations if you'd like to.

What did you say?

She's the apple of his eye.

What do you mean?

If someone is **the apple of your eye**, it means that you love them very much. It is often used to describe the way a parent feels about a child.

Why does it mean this?

The pupil (the central, black part) of the eye sometimes used to be known as the "apple". This saying suggests that the loved one is central to the person's view of the world.

Example

"He would do anything to make his daughter happy. She is **the apple of his eye**."

What did you say?

He bent over backwards.

What do you mean?

To **bend over backwards** means to try as hard as you possibly can to do something, usually to please or help someone. People sometimes say to "lean over backwards".

Example

"He has to be really careful about the food he eats, because he can't eat gluten. But the people in the restaurant were brilliant. They **bent over backwards** to make sure he had a delicious dinner."

What did you say?

They had a ball.

What do you mean?

To **have a ball** means to enjoy yourself, and have a really good time.

Why does it mean this?

The "ball" in this saying is an old-fashioned word for a dance, where people dress up and spend the evening enjoying themselves. It doesn't refer to a ball that you play with.

Example

"It was the best holiday I've ever had. I **had a ball** every day."

What did you say?

She's on the ball.

What do you mean?

To be **on the ball** means to be able to understand and deal with things well.

Why does it mean this?

In this saying, the "ball" refers to a football. A player who is "on the ball" – in other words has the ball by his or her feet – is in control of what's happening.

Example

"My grandad is nearly 90, but he's still **on the ball**. He does the crossword quicker than Mum or Dad can!"

What did you say?

The ball is in your court.

What do you mean?

If you say to someone, "**the ball is in your court**," you are telling them that it is their turn to do something or to decide what to do next before progress can be made.

Why does it mean this?

The expression refers to the game of tennis. When the ball is in someone's court (on their side of the net, in the part of the court in which they play), it is their turn to play the next stroke.

Example

"How shall we carry on from here?"

"You decide. I've told you all the changes I want made. Now **the ball is in your court**."

What did you say?

Will you start the ball rolling?

What do you mean?

To **start the ball rolling** means to start an activity, particularly if it is something with which other people will join in.

Example

"Let's all tell each other our names, where we live, and our favourite colour. Anna, will you **start the ball rolling**?"

What did you say?

That's scraping the bottom of the barrel.

What do you mean?

If someone **scrapes the bottom of the barrel**, they are forced to use or choose an idea, person or thing that is not very good, because they cannot think of or find a better alternative.

Why does it mean this?

Undrinkable, grainy bits – the "dregs" – are all that is left at the bottom of a barrel of alcohol when the good drink has gone.

Examples

"I was amazed to be picked for the spelling team. They were **scraping the bottom of the barrel** when they chose me!"

"You're being too modest! I thought you did really well."

What did you say?

He's full of beans.

What do you mean?

To be **full of beans** means to be full of energy, and be very active.

Why does it mean this?

The saying comes from a way of describing horses who were full of energy when they had been fed well.

Example

"How have the children been? They were tired this morning."

"They've not seemed tired at all. They've been **full of beans**, running around the garden all afternoon."

What did you say?

Don't spill the beans!

What do you mean?

To **spill the beans** means to give someone information, particularly information that is meant to be secret.

Why does it means this?

This expression may come from the time when the Ancient Greeks used to vote at elections by putting beans into a jar. The number of "yes" and "no" votes was kept secret until the beans were "spilled" out of the jar.

Example

"I've hidden his present in the shed. You mustn't **spill the beans** and tell him where it is!"

What did you say?

He got out of the wrong side of the bed.

What do you mean?

If you say that someone **got out of the wrong side of the bed**, it means that they are in a bad mood – usually for no obvious reason.

Why does it mean this?

This saying comes from an old superstition that if you put your left foot on the floor first when getting out of bed, you would have bad luck all day.

Example

"Jake is in a terrible mood this morning. He seems to have **got out of the wrong side of the bed**."

What did you say?

What do you mean?

If you say that something **rings a bell**, you mean that it sounds familiar, but you can't remember it exactly.

Example

"Do you remember Mrs Grant?"

"The name **rings a bell**, but I can't think who she is."

What did you say?

He drove me round the bend!

What do you mean?

To **drive someone round the bend** means to annoy or bore them so much that they feel that they are going to lose control of themselves. It has a similar meaning to driving someone up the wall (page 90).

Example

"We had to queue for ages for almost every ride at the theme park. All that waiting was **driving me round the bend!**"

What did you say?

We've missed the boat.

What do you mean?

To **miss the boat** means to miss or fail to take an opportunity to do something.

Example

"I had meant to enter that competition. But the date for entries has passed now. I **missed the boat**."

What did you say?

What do you mean?

1. If someone **rocks the boat**, they are disrupting a stable, settled situation, usually by interfering, or by trying to do things differently.

2. If someone tells you **not to rock the boat**, they mean that you shouldn't do anything that would upset or change the way things are.

Examples

1. "Everything was going fine until she came along and **rocked the boat**. Now, no one seems to get on any more."

2. "I think it's time we changed the rules, don't you?"
    "I **shouldn't rock the boat** if I were you. Everyone else seems happy with the way things are."

What did you say?

She's got a bone to pick with him.

What do you mean?

When you have **a bone to pick with someone**, it means that you are annoyed about something they have said or done, and you want to talk to them about it.

Why does it mean this?

This saying may refer to dogs squabbling over a bone that more than one of them wants to eat.

Example

"Excuse me, I've got **a bone to pick with you**! You said you were going to bring back that CD you borrowed, but you haven't!"

What did you say?

You can't judge a book by its cover.

What do you mean?

If someone says, "you **can't judge a book by its cover**," they mean that you can't tell what someone is like just by looking at them. You need to get to know them better before you decide what you think of them.

Example

"She looks unfriendly."

"I know, but she's actually just shy. She's very friendly once you get to know her. You **can't judge a book by its cover**."

What did you say?

He's too big for his boots.

What do you mean?

If you say that someone is **too big for their boots**, you are criticizing them for behaving as if they think they are more important than they are.

Example

"I liked him better before he won that prize. Since then, he's been **too big for his boots**."

What did you say?

We'll cross that bridge when we come to it.

What do you mean?

Saying that you will **cross that bridge when you come to it** means that you don't intend to waste time worrying about what might happen, but will deal with a problem if and when it does happen.

Example

"What shall we do if all the tickets are already sold by the time we get to the cinema?" she asked.

"We'll **cross that bridge when we come to it**," he replied.

What did you say?

What do you mean?

If you **take the bull by the horns**, you deal with a tricky situation in a direct, determined way.

Example

"She knew it wouldn't be easy to sort out which person should do which of the chores. Someone was bound to say that they had been given the worst job! But she **took the bull by the horns**, and just gave them a list of who had to do what."

What did you say?

She's got butterflies in her tummy.

What do you mean?

If someone is said to have **butterflies in their tummy**, it means that they are feeling nervous and jittery about something that they have to do.

Why does it mean this?

Sometimes, when you are nervous, your stomach gets a fluttery feeling, as if there were butterflies flying around in it.

Example

"Janet had the starring role in the school play. She had **butterflies in her tummy** just thinking about it."

What did you say?

I'll carry the can.

What do you mean?

To **carry the can** means to take the blame for something, even though others are also responsible.

Why does it mean this?

This was probably a military expression originally. It is thought to refer to the man chosen to carry the beer container for a group of soldiers.

Example

"Jack and Tom had been playing football near the house, where they knew they shouldn't play. When the ball broke a window, Tom decided to **carry the can**, even though it had been his younger brother who had actually kicked the ball."

What did you say?

That would be opening a can of worms!

What do you mean?

If a situation is described as being a can of worms, it is much more complicated than it seems. If someone says, "that would be **opening a can of worms**," they mean that doing something would lead to all sorts of complicated problems, and that it would be better to leave things as they are.

Example

"I wanted to find out why the video wouldn't work on the usual setting, but Dad said to leave the TV as it was. He said it would be **opening a can of worms** if we started changing the channels."

What did you say?

You're burning the candle at both ends.

What do you mean?

If you **burn the candle at both ends**, you are staying up late and getting up early.

Example

"She was exhausted. She'd been **burning the candle at both ends** for months, working late, and getting up early to revise for her exams."

What did you say?

Lay your cards on the table.

What do you mean?

To **lay** (or **put**) **your cards on the table** means not to hide the way you feel or what you plan to do, but to let other people know.

Why does it means this?

This expression refers to card games. Usually, you hide your cards from the other players, but if you lay your cards on the table face upwards, they can see which cards you have.

Example

"Look, I'll **lay my cards on the table**. We really want to buy the horse, but we can't afford it."

What did you say?

He let the cat out of the bag.

What do you mean?

To **let the cat out of the bag** means to give away a secret – usually without meaning to, or against someone else's wishes.

Why does it mean this?

This saying comes from a trick played by traders at country fairs. Pig traders sometimes tried to fool customers by giving them a sack into which they had secretly put a cat – which was worth less money than a pig. If the cat got out, the trick was discovered!

Example

"It was meant to be a surprise party, but Harry **let the cat out of the bag** by asking what time it started."

What did you say?

It's raining cats and dogs.

What do you mean?

If it is **raining cats and dogs**, it is raining heavily. This is a rather old-fashioned expression, and you are probably more likely to read this metaphor in a book than to hear it said. Now, people are more likely to say, "it's bucketing," to mean raining heavily, suggesting bucketfuls of water pouring down.

Example

"Did you enjoy the picnic yesterday?"

"No! We had to eat in the car. It was **raining cats and dogs!**"

What did you say?

He's a big cheese.

What do you mean?

If someone is described as a **big cheese**, he or she is a powerful, important person.

Why does it mean this?

The "cheese" in this expression may come from "chiz" or "cheez", a word meaning "thing" in Urdu, a language used in India. It was first used by British people when they were in India in the 19th century, and came to mean a boss.

Example

"It's a really important meeting of the Football Association. All the **big cheeses** will be there."

What did you say?

What do you mean?

Don't count your chickens (or **don't count your chickens before they are hatched**) means that it is unwise rely on something happening before it does. If you are not counting your chickens, you are waiting to see what happens.

Why does it mean this?

Not all eggs will hatch, so if you counted eggs and assumed you would have that many chickens, you might be disappointed.

Example

"I think I'll go through to the next round of the competition."
   "I hope so, but **don't count your chickens**."

What did you say?

He's got a chip on his shoulder.

What do you mean?

If someone has a **chip on their shoulder**, they are resentful about not having the benefits that they think other people have.

Why does it mean this?

Here, "chip" means a piece of wood. Apparently, men sometimes used to put a piece of wood on their shoulder, hoping that someone would knock it off – and give them an excuse to fight!

Example

"She's got a huge **chip on her shoulder**, because she doesn't go to the same school as most of her friends. She is worried that they think they are better than her because of it. Of course, they don't think that. She just imagines they do."

What did you say?

That's the way the cookie crumbles.

What do you mean?

If someone says, "**that's the way the cookie crumbles**," they mean that you have to accept the way things have happened, even if they haven't worked out as you wanted.

Example

"But that's not fair! They got three goes and I only got two!"

"**That's the way the cookie crumbles**. Don't worry. Next time, you might get the extra go."

What did you say?

What do you mean?

Too many cooks spoil the broth means that an activity or plan goes wrong because too many people are involved in it.

Why does it mean this?

Broth is a soup. If lots of people are involved in deciding on how to make it, it could spoil the taste.

Example

"We were all trying to decorate the room together, but it ended up looking a bit of mess, as we all like different styles and colours."

　　"Too many cooks spoil the broth."

　　"Exactly."

What did you say?

She was sent to Coventry.

What do you mean?

Sending someone to Coventry is an unkind way of showing disapproval by ignoring them and not speaking to them.

Why does it mean this?

The saying is thought to come from a time when soldiers were sent to an English city called Coventry, where they were not popular, and so were not spoken to by the local people.

Example

"His brothers were very angry with him for taking their computer games without asking. They **sent him to Coventry** for the rest of the afternoon. But at tea-time, we talked about it, apologies were made, and everyone was friends again."

What did you say?

It's not my cup of tea.

What do you mean?

If something is **not your cup of tea**, you don't like it very much. It's a way of saying that something is not to your taste.

Example

"I listened to that band's new album, but it's **not really my cup of tea.** I prefer their old stuff."

What did you say?

What do you mean?

To **call it a day** means to stop doing something, usually because you are tired or bored, or because you realize that continuing is unlikely to achieve the result you would like.

Example

"I went in about 20 shops to look for the video he wanted, then I decided to **call it a day**."

What did you say?

What do you mean?

If you **put all your eggs in one basket**, you are putting all your effort, money or resources into one thing. The danger is that if that thing is unsuccessful, you risk losing everything.

Why does it means this?

If you put all your eggs in one basket, and you drop the basket, you risk breaking all the eggs.

Example

"I'm just going concentrate on my chemistry."

"But what if you don't get accepted to do chemistry at university? **Don't put all your eggs in one basket**. You really need to work hard at all your science subjects."

What did you say?

I'm walking on eggshells.

What do you mean?

If you are **walking** (or **treading**) **on eggshells**, you are being very careful about what you do or say in case you upset someone, who you think is being over-sensitive or moody.

Example

"She is very easily upset at the moment, and starts to cry if she thinks you're criticizing her – even when you're not."

"I know. I feel I'm **walking on eggshells** whenever I'm with her."

What did you say?

She was thrown in at the deep end.

What do you mean?

To be **thrown in at the deep end** means to be given a difficult new job or task, without any preparation.

Why does it mean this?

The expression refers to the deep end of a swimming pool. If you were thrown in at the deep end of the pool, you would have to swim – or you would sink.

Example

"My Dad started his new job this week. He doesn't mind being **thrown in at the deep end**. He says he'll have to learn fast and show his boss he can do it!"

"He's brave!"

What did you say?

They can't make ends meet.

What do you mean?

If you can't **make ends meet** or you find it difficult to **make ends meet**, it means you don't have enough money to buy food, clothes and other things you need.

Why does it mean this?

The original saying was "to make both ends meet at the end of the year". This meant to only spend as much money each year as you earned.

Example

"My sister is at university. She's got lots of studying to do, but she has to do a part-time job as well, or she can't **make ends meet**."

What did you say?

What do you mean?

To **find your feet** means to come to feel confident in an unfamiliar situation – such as starting a new job or a new school, or learning a new skill.

Example

"She's just started at secondary school. At first she found it quite difficult, because the place is so large, and there are so many new subjects and different ways of doing things. But she's **found her feet** now, and is really enjoying it."

What did you say?

You've really landed on your feet!

What do you mean?

To **land** (or **fall**) **on your feet** means to be in a good situation through luck rather than effort or planning.

Why does it mean this?

This saying may refer to the belief that cats always land on their feet, without coming to any harm, whenever and wherever they fall.

Example

"He really **fell on his feet** when he went to live in Scotland. He found a lovely house to live in, and got a great new job straight away."

What did you say?

What do you mean?

To **sit on the fence** means to not give a definite opinion about something, or not say which side you support in a conflict.

Why does it mean this?

It's as if there is a fence separating two sides. If you sit on the fence, you don't choose to be with one side or the other.

Example

"The five of them were trying to decide what to do. Jack and Mary wanted to go to the cinema. Sean and Mark wanted to go swimming. Christine **sat on the fence**, as usual, and said she couldn't decide!"

What did you say?

Keep your fingers crossed!

What do you mean?

To say you are going to **keep your fingers crossed**, or **cross your fingers** means that you are wishing for success or good luck. Saying "**fingers crossed**" can mean "good luck" or "with luck".

Why does it mean this?
Making the sign of the cross (a Christian symbol) with the fingers was thought to give protection against the devil or bad luck.

Examples

1. "I hope the exam goes well. I'll **keep my fingers crossed** for you!"

2. "It's your turn now! **Fingers crossed!**"

What did you say?

You've put your finger on it!

What do you mean?

1. If you **put your finger on something**, it means that you can identify the reason for something or realize the exact cause of a problem.

2. If you **can't put your finger on something**, you can't explain something exactly.

Examples

1. "Dr Watson couldn't think of any motive for the crime. But Sherlock Holmes **put his finger on it** straight away!"

2. "I saw Sally at the shops yesterday. There was something different about her, but I **couldn't put my finger on it**."

What did you say?

She's got him wrapped around her little finger.

What do you mean?

If you can **wrap someone around your little finger**, it means that you can persuade them to do anything you want. People sometimes use the verb "twist" rather than "wrap".

Example

"His parents spoiled him terribly. He could **wrap them around his little finger**."

What did you say?

What do you mean?

To **play with fire** means to do something that could get you into trouble.

Why does it mean this?

Playing with fire is very dangerous.

Example

"You're **playing with fire** if you get involved with that gang."

What did you say?

He's a big fish in a small pond.

What do you mean?

If someone is described as a **big fish in a small pond**, it means that they have an important position, but only within a small group or organization. The saying suggests that if they were in a bigger group, they would be considered much less important.

Example

"How is Janet enjoying secondary school?"

"Well, she likes it now, but it's so different from her primary. It took her a while to get used to the change from being a **big fish in a small pond** to being a humble first year."

What did you say?

What do you mean?

If someone is sad because their relationship with a girlfriend or boyfriend has come to an end, people might try to comfort them by saying, "there are **plenty more fish in the sea**," meaning that there are lots of other people to find happiness with.

Example

"She's still crying about Thomas telling her he didn't want to go out with her any more. I told her there were **plenty more fish in the sea**, but I don't think it helped."

"It was good of you to try and make her feel better, but I think she'll need more time before she can start to be interested in anyone else."

What did you say?

I've got a frog in my throat!

What do you mean?

If you have a **frog in your throat** it means that you can't speak clearly because your throat is dry or hoarse for the moment.

Why does it mean this?

In the Middle Ages, people believed that if you drank water that contained frog spawn, the frogs would grow inside your body. A sore throat or cough was thought to be caused by the frogs trying to escape!

Example

"Peter had to stop in the middle of his speech, because he had a **frog in his throat**. He had a sip of water and he was fine again."

What did you say?

They kept moving the goalposts.

What do you mean?

To **move the goalposts** means to change the aims, the limits or the rules of a situation or activity, with the effect that other people are confused and don't know what is expected of them.

Why does it mean this?

If you moved the actual goalposts in a game such as football, it would be confusing, and it would be difficult to score any goals.

Example

"I thought she just wanted 10 correct answers before we could move on to the next level, but now she says she wants 15! If she keeps **moving the goalposts**, I don't know when I'll finish."

What did you say?

You're teaching your grandmother to suck eggs!

What do you mean?

If you are **teaching your grandmother to suck eggs**, you are telling someone (not necessarily your grandmother!) how to do something that they already know more about than you do.

Example

"That's right. If you measure from that corner to this corner, then that corner to that corner, you can work out how much wallpaper we need."

"Don't try to **teach your grandmother to suck eggs**! I've been doing this job for years!"

What did you say?

What do you mean?

1. To **lend** (or **give**) **a hand** means to help someone.

2. You can also say someone **needs a hand** if they need help.

Examples

1. "Can someone **lend me a hand** with these shopping bags please? They are too heavy for me to carry by myself."

2. "It looks as if Jim **needs a hand** with tying his shoelaces. Will you help him please Sally?"

What did you say?

She flew off the handle.

What do you mean?

If someone **flies off the handle**, they suddenly become very angry and appear out of control.

Why does it mean this?

This saying refers to an axe head coming loose and flying off its handle as it is being swung.

Example

"He had too much work to do, and was very stressed. But when I suggested taking a holiday, he **flew off the handle** and shouted at me, saying that he didn't have time!"

What did you say?

Keep it under your hat.

What do you mean?

If you are told something and then asked to "**keep it under your hat**", you are being asked not to tell anyone else.

Example

"I'm looking for a new job, but I don't want my boss to find out yet. So, please **keep it under your hat**."

What did you say?

Let's bury the hatchet.

What do you mean?

To **bury the hatchet** means to make up and become friends again after an argument.

Why does it mean this?
Native American tribes used to bury a tomahawk (a type of hatchet or axe) as a sign of peace after a conflict was over.

Example
"You and Harry seem to be getting on better these days."

"Yes. We used to argue all the time, but now we've **buried the hatchet**."

What did you say?

He has his head in the clouds.

What do you mean?

If someone has his or her **head in the clouds**, it means that they spend their time imagining things that they would like to happen, rather than paying attention to things that actually are happening.

Example

"While her friends settled down to dance practice, she always had her **head in the clouds**, dreaming of the day when she would be a famous ballerina."

What did you say?

She can do that standing on her head.

What do you mean?

To be able to **do something standing on your head** means
you can do it very easily, without any effort.

Why does it mean this?

The saying suggests that you find something so easy that you
could do it even while doing something else, such as a headstand.

Example

"His new teacher asked him to do what she thought was a
difficult exercise – to work out how many in the class were
younger than the average age. He could **do it standing on his
head**! He had always been good at maths."

What did you say?

What do you mean?

If you are **speaking off the top of your head**, you are saying something without thinking about it much or considering it carefully, so that what you say may not be correct.

Example

"How many lambs were born this year at your Dad's farm?"

"About 20, I think. But I'm **speaking off the top of my head**. It may be more."

What did you say?

She will bite your head off!

What do you mean?

If you say that someone **bites your head off**, you mean they speak to you in an angry, snappy way – usually because they are bad-tempered, annoyed or perhaps worried about something.

Example

" Are you ready to go?" she asked.

"Does it look like it?" he shouted angrily.

"OK, don't **bite my head off**! I was only asking!"

What did you say?

He's burying his head in the sand.

What do you mean?

To **bury your head in the sand** means to try to pretend something unpleasant isn't happening, because you don't want to have to deal with it.

Why does it mean this?

People used to think that ostriches buried their head in the sand so that they couldn't see a dangerous situation.

Example

"You have to do something about this problem. Don't **bury your head in the sand**, and hope it will go away – because it won't! You must deal with it. I'll help you if I can."

What did you say?

What do you mean?

To get information **straight from the horse's mouth** means to learn about it directly from the person who knows most about the subject.

Example

"It's not just a rumour that there is going to be a new hockey team. I heard it **straight from the horse's mouth**."
    "What, did the coach tell you himself?"
    "Yes."

What did you say?

What do you mean?

To **break the ice** means to do something that helps people to relax and feel at ease, especially when they have just met.

Why does it mean this?

The saying is thought to come from the act of breaking the ice around a ship before it can set sail.

Example

"How did you get on at your new group?"

"We all felt a bit embarrassed, because it was the first time we had met. But Tom **broke the ice** by getting us all to say our names and what our favourite TV programmes were."

What did you say?

Take a leaf out of his book.

What did you mean?

If you **take a leaf out of someone's book**, you copy the way they behave, because they set a good example.

Why does it mean this?

In this saying, a "leaf" means a page in a book. Imagine the book is a play, and the "leaf" is a page containing someone's script. If you had the same script as that person, you would act like them.

Example

"You should **take a leaf out of Peter's book**. When he finds things difficult, he tries his best. And when he finds things easy, he doesn't boast about his achievements."

What did you say?

He's turned over a new leaf.

What do you mean?

If you **turn over a new leaf**, you start behaving in a better way than before.

Why does it mean this?

Once again (see page 62), "leaf" means the page of a book. It's as if you were starting afresh on a new page.

Example

"Last term he was very cheeky and often got into trouble. But since the holidays, he seems to have **turned over a new leaf**. He works hard and is a really helpful member of the class."

What did you say?

You're pulling my leg.

What do you mean?

1. To **pull someone's leg** means to tell them something that isn't true, as a joke. People sometimes call this sort of a joke a leg-pull.

2. If someone **has their leg pulled**, it can also mean that they are being teased about something.

Examples

1. "He said he'd met Madonna when he was in London. But I knew he was **pulling my leg**."

2. "She was always **having her leg pulled** about her new boyfriend. I think her friends were actually jealous."

What did you say?

Let's draw a line under it.

What do you mean?

To **draw a line under something** means to put a bad situation into the past, and stop worrying about it or talking about it any more. (To draw the line *at* something has a different meaning. It means to refuse to do something.)

Why does it mean this?

If you draw a line under a piece of work, it shows that you have finished with it, and are moving on to the next thing.

Example

"Stop arguing. It's time to **draw a line under your quarrel** and get on with enjoying the rest of the holiday."

What did you say?

He needs a square meal.

What do you mean?

A **square meal** is a good, filling meal.

Why does it mean this?

This saying probably comes from the square wooden plates off which sailors used to eat their meals.

Example

"I'm feeling a bit weak and hungry."

"You'll feel better once you've got a **square meal** inside you."

What did you say?

minds

He's always changing his mind.

What do you mean?

To **change your mind** means to change the way you think about something, or to have a different plan from previously. It's a bit like "to change your tune" (page 89), but while that suggests changing an opinion or attitude, this means simply changing the way you feel about something or deciding to do something different. You can use this to refer to others or yourself.

Example

"I didn't expect to see you here! I thought you were going to the cinema this afternoon."

"I know. But it's such a lovely day, I **changed my mind**. I felt like being out in the sunshine."

What did you say?

She's over the moon.

What do you mean?

If you are **over the moon**, you are very happy about something. It's a similar saying to "on top of the world" (page 100), but suggests that you are happy about something in particular.

Example

"I hear you passed your violin exam. Well done!"
"Thanks. I'm **over the moon** about it."

What did you say?

She'll have to face the music.

What do you mean?

To **face the music** means to take responsibility for doing something wrong, and to prepare yourself for criticism or punishment.

Example

"He knew he shouldn't have used his brother's bike without asking, and it was his fault that he'd got a nasty scratch on it. There was no way he could hide the scratch, so he decided that he would just have to **face the music**."

What did you say?

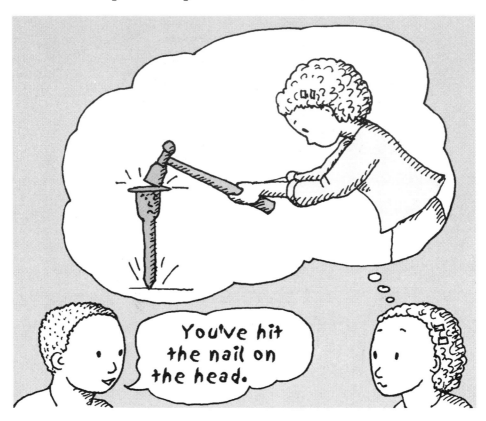

You've hit the nail on the head.

What do you mean?

To **hit the nail on the head** means to describe a situation precisely or to give exactly the right answer or explanation. "To put your finger on it" (page 43) has a similar meaning.

Example

"I think the main problem in this area is the lack of a good bus service."

"You're right. You've **hit the nail on the head**."

What did you say?

What do you mean?

If you describe a plan or an idea as **pie in the sky**, you mean that you think it is unlikely to happen.

Example

"She says her plan is to live in London and set up her own hairdressing business. But it's **pie in the sky**. She's only just started as an assistant at the local salon."

What did you say?

We had to eat humble pie.

What do you mean?

To **eat humble pie** means to admit that you were wrong, and apologize, particularly if this is humiliating.

Why does it mean this?

The "umbles" are the insides of an animal, such as the heart and liver. In the past, noble people ate the best meat, while their servants (humble people) ate the "umbles" in a pie. The words "umbles" and "humble" have become mixed in this saying.

Example

"He said that the other player cheated. When he was proved wrong, he had to **eat humble pie**, and make a public apology."

What did you say?

She's got a lot on her plate.

What do you mean?

If someone has **a lot on their plate**, they have a lot of work to do, or a lot of problems to deal with. To have enough on your plate means the same thing.

Example

"I wouldn't ask him to do any more work. He's got **a lot on his plate** already."

What did you say?

He's been given the sack.

What did you mean?

To be **given the sack**, or to **get the sack** means to be be dismissed from your job (to be told you have lost your job).

Why does it mean this?

Workers used to carry the tools of their trade in a bag, which they would leave with their employer while they worked for him. When the job was finished, they would be given the bag back. The saying originated in France, where "sac" is the word for bag.

Example

"He was late for work three times last week. He'll be **given the sack** if he doesn't start coming in on time."

What did you say?

She's come out of her shell.

What do you mean?

To **come out of your shell** means to become less shy than before, and to start being more sociable.

Why does it mean this?

When shellfish and snails are frightened, they hide inside their shells. When they feel safe, they come out again.

Example

"She was very shy when she first went to her new school, but she soon **came out of her shell**."

What did you say?

Get your skates on!

What do you mean?

To **get your skates on** means to hurry up.

Why does it mean this?

You can go faster when you are wearing ice skates or roller skates.

Example

"We'd better **get our skates on**, or we'll miss the start of the film."

What did you say?

There's a skeleton in the cupboard!

What do you mean?

If someone has a **skeleton in their cupboard**, they have a secret which would embarrass them or would cause a scandal if it were known about.

Example

"The newspapers used to say how wonderful he was, but now they are determined to find a **skeleton in his cupboard**. That's the problem with being a celebrity, I suppose."

What did you say?

I've got something up my sleeve.

What do you mean?

If someone has **something up their sleeve**, they have a plan or a secret idea that they think will help to achieve something.

Why does it mean this?

A cheating card player might hide cards up his sleeve, and slip them into his hand when it would help him to win.

Example

"We've tried and tried to get her to join the team. I can't think of anything else we could say to persuade her."

"Well, I've got **something up my sleeve** that might help. I've arranged it so that we get time off school to practise."

What did you say?

He's a snake in the grass.

What do you mean?

If someone is a **snake in the grass**, they are pretending to be friendly, but are really intending to do harm.

Example

"He's a real **snake in the grass**. He pretended to be interested in our ideas, but he was really finding out information about us that he could use to get us into trouble."

What did you say?

Pull your socks up!

What do you mean?

To **pull your socks up** means to try harder or to improve your behaviour.

Example

"Jane was very clever, but she didn't like to do school work. Her teacher told her that she would have to **pull her socks up** if she was going to do well in her exams."

What did you say?

It's the last straw.

What do you mean?

If you say that something is the **last straw** or the **final straw**, you mean that one final thing in a series of difficulties has made you feel that the situation is intolerable.

Example

"The weather was terrible. Our hotel room was small and damp. Then there was a power cut, which they said would last all day! That was the **last straw**. We came home!"

What did you say?

You've drawn the short straw.

What do you mean?

If you **draw the short straw**, it means that you have been chosen to do a task that no one wants to do.

Why does it mean this?

This expression comes from a way of drawing lots to decide on something by chance. A person holds several pieces of straw. One straw is short, but they are held so that they all look the same length. Whoever pulls out the short straw loses.

Example

"Are you working at Christmas?"
"Yes. I've **drawn the short straw** this year."

What did you say?

It was the straw that broke the camel's back.

What do you mean?

The **straw that breaks the camel's back** has a very similar meaning to "the last straw" (see page 81). It refers to something happening which finally makes you unable to cope with a situation.

Why does it mean this?

Here the image is of a camel being used as a beast of burden. One final thing makes it reach the limit of what it can carry.

Example

"Julie's been ill, and she's been practising really hard, so she's very tired. When they brought her piano exam forward a day, it was the **straw that broke the camel's back**."

What did you say?

What do you mean?

If you say "it's **swings and roundabouts**" about a situation or a decision, you mean that there are both advantages and disadvantages in doing something one way rather than another. This expression is a shortened form of a proverb (a wise saying): "what you lose on the swings you gain on the roundabouts".

Example

"Shall we walk or take the car?"

"It's **swings and roundabouts** really. We'd obviously get there quicker by car, but it could take a long time to find a parking space, and there could be so much traffic that it might be quicker to walk home rather than drive."

What did you say?

Hold your tongue!

What do you mean?

1. To **hold your tongue** means to keep silent.

2. To **bite your tongue** is similar: it means to keep quiet about something for the moment, because it wouldn't be the right time or place to speak.

Examples

1. "It would help if you could **hold your tongue** for just one more minute until I've finished trying to tune in the television. Then we can talk about it."

2. "I wanted to tell her that I'd just seen Andrew, but I decided to **bite my tongue** for the moment."

What did you say?

What do you mean?

When someone says that something is **on the tip of their tongue**, they mean that they can't quite remember something, such as a name or the answer to a question, even though they are sure that they do know it.

Example

"What's the name of that guitarist we were talking about yesterday?"

"Oh dear, I can't remember. It's **on the tip of my tongue**. I know – it begins with V – Valley no, Valiant. That's it, Valiant."

What did you say?

She's a bit long in the tooth!

What do you mean?

To be **long in the tooth** means to be old.

Why does it mean this?

People's teeth look longer as they get older, because gums recede (shrink).

Example

"I'm a bit too **long in the tooth** to want to start a new career now."

What did you say?

Speech bubble: He's barking up the wrong tree.

What do you mean?

If someone is **barking up the wrong tree**, they have the wrong idea about something, or they misunderstand the situation.

Why does it mean this?

The expression comes from using hunting dogs to bark up at a particular tree to show that an animal is hiding in it. Sometimes they bark up the wrong tree.

Example

"They thought that she didn't want to come to the disco because she didn't like dancing. But they were **barking up the wrong tree**. It was because she didn't like the flashing lights."

What did you say?

What do you mean?

To **change your tune** means to have a different attitude towards something or someone, or to have a different opinion than before. It is a bit like "to change your mind" (page 67). However, you would use this saying only to describe other people, not to refer to yourself.

Example

"She used to say that soap operas were really boring, but now she's **changed her tune**. She loves watching them."

What did you say?

She drove me up the wall!

What do you mean?

To **drive someone up the wall** means to annoy them greatly. It has a similar meaning to "driving someone round the bend" (page 12).

Example

"She plays her music really loudly until two in the morning. It **drives me up the wall!**"

What did you say?

It's water off a duck's back!

What do you mean?

If you say that something (usually a criticism, a telling-off or an insult) is **water off a duck's back** or like water off a duck's back to someone, you mean that it has no effect on them.

Why does it mean this?

Ducks have specially oily feathers to stop them absorbing water when they are swimming. Water doesn't make them wet – it flows straight off them.

Example

"I must have told her a hundred times that she mustn't do that, but it's **water off a duck's back**! She just goes on doing it."

What did you say?

That's water under the bridge.

What do you mean?

1. If you say "That's **water under the bridge**," you mean that it's something that happened in the past, and it's not worth thinking about or worrying about any more.

2. "**A lot of water has gone** (or **flowed** or **passed**) **under the bridge** since..." means that lots has happened since a particular event or situation.

Examples

1. "Forget about that row. It's **water under the bridge**."

2. "**A lot of water has gone under the bridge** since we last met."

What did you say?

He's feeling under the weather.

What do you mean?

If someone is **feeling under the weather**, it means that they are not feeling well. People often say, "**feeling a bit under the weather**."

Example

"Do you fancy coming to the skateboard park this evening?"

"No. I think I'll stay in and go to bed early. I'm **feeling a bit under the weather**."

What did you say?

You have to pull your weight.

What do you mean?

1. To **pull your weight** means to work as hard as everybody else involved in the same task.

2. It is often used in the negative, to suggest that someone isn't working as hard as they should be.

Examples

1. "Putting on this performance is fun, but it's also hard work. Everyone has to **pull their weight** if we are going to succeed."

2. "She's not **pulling her weight**."
   "I know. She'd rather sit around chatting than do any work."

What did you say?

What do you mean?

If you say that someone is a **wolf in sheep's clothing**, you mean that he or she is pretending to be nice or harmless, but is really nastier or more dangerous than he or she appears.

Why does it mean this?

One of Aesop's fables tells the story of a wolf who disguises himself in a sheep's fleece. He gets fenced in with the sheep without being noticed. Once there, he attacks and eats the sheep.

Example

"I wanted to warn you about Tim. He seems sweet, but he's a **wolf in sheep's clothing**. He'll do anything to get that job."

What did you say?

We're not out of the woods yet.

What do you mean?

If you are **not out of the woods**, you are still having problems or are still in a difficult situation.

Example

"I hear Alan has been very ill. How is he now?"

"He's much better than he was, but he's **not out of the woods** yet."

What did you say?

He's pulling the wool over your eyes.

What do you mean?

To **pull the wool over someone's eyes** means to deceive them – to make them believe something which isn't true.

Why does it mean this?

The wigs men used to wear in the past were sometimes called "wool". A robber might pull the "wool" over a victim's eyes, so that he would not be able to see who was robbing him.

Example

"Over-18s only allowed, Juliet. I know you've got lots of make-up on, but I know how old you are, so you can't **pull the wool over my eyes**! Come back in three years!"

What did you say?

I couldn't get a word in edgeways.

What do you mean?

If you can't **get a word in edgeways**, it means that someone else is talking so much that you have no opportunity to speak.

Example

"She was so excited about it that she just couldn't seem to stop talking. Nobody else could **get a word in edgeways**."

What did you say?

What do you mean?

To **take the words right out of someone's mouth** means to say something that they were just going to say. (Sometimes people leave out the word "right".)

Example

"It's such a sunny day, do you feel like going for a walk?"

"You **took the words right out of my mouth**! I was just going to ask you exactly the same thing."

What did you say?

He's on top of the world.

What do you mean?

To be **on top of the world** is to be really happy. It has a similar meaning to "over the moon" (page 68).

Example

"She'd had such a good birthday, she felt **on top of the world**."

What did you say?

cat the
deck

What did you mean?

Divide the
pack of cards
in two.

What did you say?

What did you mean?

To **keep your eyes peeled** means to look "carefully" or search thoroughly for something.

Example

"I have no idea where my wallet is. Would you please help me find it? **Keep your eyes peeled** for it."

What did you say?

What did you mean?

What did you say?

What did you mean?

What did you say?

What did you mean?

What did you say?

What did you mean?

Appendix I

For parents and teachers: a guide to helping children with Asperger Syndrome to understand what we mean

Children with autistic spectrum disorders, including those with Asperger Syndrome, tend to understand and use language literally. They expect words to mean what they seem to say, and can be confused and distressed when this isn't the case.

Imagine this scene. A classroom of 25 eight-year-olds. The teacher is trying to make sure they finish their work before the bell goes for lunch. Most of the children are concentrating, even though this necessarily means discussing the topic with their classmates. There is a hum of collaborative conversation as they attend to the task in hand.

One boy, whose worksheet is almost empty, isn't writing or talking, but chewing his pencil and looking out of the window at the workmen carrying out restoration work in the playground. The teacher walks over to him: "Simon," she says sharply, "you've hardly started. You'd better pull your socks up if you're going to finish in time!" Simon looks shocked and flustered. He bends down, and pulls his socks up. "Simon!" the teacher shouts, "I will have no insolence in my class."

What has happened here?

Simon has Asperger Syndrome, but this has not been diagnosed. The teacher (who perhaps wouldn't be the teacher of choice for any child) is as unaware of his needs as he is of the meaning of her metaphorical instruction. Simon thought he was doing as he was told, even though he couldn't understand why she wanted him to pull his socks up. He had heard what she said, but he didn't understand what she meant. She, in turn, mistook his literal interpretation as insolence. He misunderstood her. She misunderstood him. They both responded inappropriately.

It is important to remember that the social and communication issues central to autism and Asperger Syndrome are two-way. Those of us without an autistic spectrum disorder, who are able to make sense of the social world with little conscious effort, can help those with impaired social understanding. But we first have to be sensitive to their needs. We would hope that once Simon had been diagnosed as having Asperger Syndrome, this (luckily imaginary) teacher would become more aware of what was a real problem for him, and change her tune (see page 89).

Finding metaphorical language difficult to understand may not sound like a big thing, but it can be. If you told a child with Asperger Syndrome that someone had had their head bitten off, for example, they might be extremely frightened. One child was worried to hear that school was "breaking up" – he thought the building was falling down. Another boy with Asperger Syndrome was absolutely terrified when a friend's father told him philosophically, "At the end of the day, we're all going to die." Understandably for a literal thinker, he thought that this meant everyone was going to die that night, and rang his parents in a complete panic.

It is so easy to use phrases such as "at the end of the day" without thinking. But if you know you are talking to a child with Asperger Syndrome, simply making the effort to choose words with more care can make a huge difference.

Taking language literally encompasses more than misinterpreting metaphors. It extends to taking words at their face value, and not inferring the intended meaning behind questions such as "Can you count to ten?" One child, when asked this during an assessment simply replied, "Yes." She did not recognize the fact that she was expected to demonstrate her ability – because she had not explicitly been asked to do so.

Beware of suggesting to a child that he has a choice when he doesn't. For example, if you asked a child with Asperger Syndrome, "Would you like to sit down now?" when you actually meant, "I would like you to sit down now," the child might interpret what you say literally, and think you really were offering a choice (when you weren't). Such misunderstanding could lead the child to respond in an unexpected way, which in turn could be misinterpreted as deliberate disobedience or cheek – for which the child might wrongly be reprimanded.

Language that does not mean what it says can add to the burden of stress experienced by children with Asperger Syndrome. Yet many of these stresses are drastically decreased if the people in a child's life – family, friends and professionals – are aware and sympathetic enough to try to see the world through their eyes, and teach them things that most other people understand intuitively.

Take time to think about the words you use, and explain what you mean. Try to reduce the opportunities for misinterpretation. If the child is looking down, for example, and you want them to look straight ahead, saying "Look straight ahead" is more likely to get the required response than "Look up", which can be interpreted literally as look "up" – i.e. upwards. It might help to use more nouns in your speech than you usually do: saying "Sit in the chair" is clearer than "Sit down".

Literality of thinking makes it difficult for a child with Asperger Syndrome to recognize the significance or meaning of tone, inflection and emphasis in spoken language. As a class exercise, teachers could introduce the idea that emphasising different words in a sentence can change the sentence's meaning. Take a sentence such as "She didn't say that". You could write the sentence on the board, changing the word emphasis each time:

She didn't say that.
She **didn't** say that.
She didn't **say** that.
She didn't say **that**.

Read out (and/or get the children to read out) the sentences, emphasising the selected word, and discuss the different meanings that can be inferred. (Parents could do similar activities at home.) Practise with this and other sentences, asking the children to put the emphasis on the correct word to express a particular meaning that you have given. For example, ask the children to say "I don't want that book" to mean

a.   I don't want that particular book.

b.   I don't want that book myself, but someone else might.

Literal thinking extends to misunderstanding irony and sarcasm, which are likely to be lost on a child with Asperger Syndrome. Saying "Great!" in a sarcastic tone, for example, when you actually mean the opposite, may be misinterpreted literally, and the child may think you're pleased. Again, this confusion may have consequences such as the child being seen as deliberately obtuse or naughty.

Although using sarcasm with children who have Asperger Syndrome is usually inappropriate, we should not ignore the fact that people do use it. We can explain to a child what sarcasm and irony are, and how, why and when they are used. We can teach them how the tone of voice in which words are said affects the words' meaning. Try saying things in different tones, and getting the child to guess whether you mean what you say or mean the opposite. Model accompanying body language and facial expression, and point them out to the child, explaining that these are clues to the meaning behind the words. Get them to practise saying things in different tones. Watch videos together, and discuss things such as tone of voice, irony and sarcasm.

Our conversational language is often peppered with metaphors, but some parents and professionals have avoided using them for fear of confusing or scaring the child with autism and Asperger Syndrome. This can't prepare the child for the real world. And anyway, metaphorical language can be fun. If non-literal language is presented, explained and explored in a relaxed way, it can enrich these children's understanding of the world, as well as enriching their own use of language, and making it less formal.

Helping children with Asperger Syndrome to recognize and even enjoy metaphors can have the added bonus of encouraging more general flexibility of thought – if they gain enjoyable experience of thinking about words, images, and meanings from more than one angle. Inflexibility of thought, and feeling threatened by change and alternative views, is very much part of autism and Asperger Syndrome. Learning to "loosen up" language, and acknowledge that words can have different meanings depending on how and when they are used, may help children to tolerate change and to appreciate other people's perspectives.

Helping children with Asperger Syndrome to understand what we mean also has an added bonus for those of us without an autistic spectrum disorder. Each time we try to see the world through their eyes, or hear the world through their ears, and try to adapt accordingly, we take a step closer to understanding and appreciating their experience. This in turn enriches our own experience – because, as Tony Attwood writes in an eloquent metaphor, individuals with Asperger Syndrome "are a bright thread in the rich tapestry of life". As the mother of a child with Asperger Syndrome, I know what he means.

Appendix 2

For parents and teachers: ideas for using this book

This book can be used one-to-one with a child with Asperger Syndrome. Children with an autistic spectrum disorder tend to learn best with visual supports. So the book has been specifically tailored to their needs by pointing out visually – through the use of speech and thought bubbles – the idea that someone can say and mean one thing, and that another person can interpret the words in a way the speaker didn't intend.

As you work with the child, you can stress that misinterpretation doesn't mean the listener isn't clever, just that he needs an explanation. Tell them it's OK to ask if they don't understand what someone has said. You may point out (if the child knows he has Asperger Syndrome) that people with Asperger Syndrome tend to think literally, but that most people sometimes use metaphors. Having learned some of the metaphors, the child can practise using them.

Since no one is born knowing what metaphors mean, children without an autistic spectrum disorder need to learn them too, so teachers can use the book as a starting point for class discussions, activities and projects on this theme. Here are a few ideas:

○ Play "choose the metaphor" game: make up situations and get the children to choose (from a multiple choice list) the appropriate metaphor. For example:

If someone is feeling really happy, they are...

   a. feeling under the weather

   b. on top of the world

   c. big-headed.

o Ask the children to write stories using a repertoire of metaphors.

o Making sure that the child with Asperger Syndrome doesn't find it too difficult or threatening, you could ask the children to role play scenarios and conversations in which some of the metaphors could be used.